OAKLEY

D0536949

For Vanessa, my splendid collaborator ~ J. H.

For Mum ~ T. F.

Sleepy Places

Judy Hindley

illustrated by

Tor Freeman

CANDLEWICK PRESS
CAMBRIDGE, MASSACHUSETTS

When you're yawning and nodding and flopping,
and ready to fall in a heap,
where do you choose for a nap or a snooze —
where is your favorite place to sleep?

A rabbit sleeps
tight in its
burrow;

a bird
snuggles
down in
a tree.

SNORE

A frog takes
a snooze in
the ooze of a pond;

a rose makes
a bed for a bee.

Do you suppose you
could drowse in a rose,

or snooze in the ooze

like a frog?

A cat can nap on somebody's hat; a bear curls up in a cave.

A fish may dream in
   the reeds of a stream;

a seal lolls about
   on a wave. . . .

Can you imagine what dreams you'd have,

lolling about on a wave?

A swift can sleep
    on the wing as it flies;

a horse
can sleep on
the hoof;

bats hang
upside
down from
their toes,
in rows
upon rows
in the roof.

If you were a bat,
you'd sleep like that,
upside down
in the roof!

A pup likes to sleep

    in a quivering heap,

    with a bundle of sisters and brothers.

Kangaroo joeys tuck themselves up in pockets attached to their mothers.

But what about you?

What place do you choose —
what sleepy place
for a nap
or a snooze?

A nest of cushions,

a cave of quilts,

a bundle of pillows . . .

a crib,

a buggy?

A hammock,

a sofa,

a box,

a rug,

a comfy lap,

so soft and snug?

Or would you choose your own little bed,
with your own little blanket and pillow,

and kisses and stories and teddies and things,
and somebody tucking you in?

Oh, yes –

we each have a

favorite sleepy place. . . .

Good night.

Good night.

Good night!